THE UNTOLD LIFE OF MY SAGE MOTHER

DEEPAK GUPTA

Copyright © Deepak Gupta
All Rights Reserved.

This book has been self-published with all reasonable efforts taken to make the material error-free by the author. No part of this book shall be used, reproduced in any manner whatsoever without written permission from the author, except in the case of brief quotations embodied in critical articles and reviews.

The Author of this book is solely responsible and liable for its content including but not limited to the views, representations, descriptions, statements, information, opinions and references ["Content"]. The Content of this book shall not constitute or be construed or deemed to reflect the opinion or expression of the Publisher or Editor. Neither the Publisher nor Editor endorse or approve the Content of this book or guarantee the reliability, accuracy or completeness of the Content published herein and do not make any representations or warranties of any kind, express or implied, including but not limited to the implied warranties of merchantability, fitness for a particular purpose. The Publisher and Editor shall not be liable whatsoever for any errors, omissions, whether such errors or omissions result from negligence, accident, or any other cause or claims for loss or damages of any kind, including without limitation, indirect or consequential loss or damage arising out of use, inability to use, or about the reliability, accuracy or sufficiency of the information contained in this book.

Made with ♥ on the Notion Press Platform
www.notionpress.com

*Dedicated to the strongest person I know, my Mother, **Poonam Rani**.*

Look Mom, I have written this book for you as I promised. Will you read it? Sigh! Tears! Love! Silence! Pain! Strong! Hope! Friends! Life!

Hope for the Fighters!

Peace for the Survivors!

Prayers for the Taken!

Contents

Note For The Readers	vii
Acknowledgement And Appreciation	ix
Prologue	xiii
1. 17th May 2022	1
2. 11th & 12th June 2022	6
3. 22nd June 2022	9
4. 4th July 2022	11
5. 5th July 2022 - The Next Day	15
6. 1st August 2022	23
7. 14th August 2022	28
8. 15th & 16th August 2022	30
9. 17th August 2022	33
10. 19th August 2022- Janmashtami	36
11. 20th – 22th August 2022	39
12. 23rd August 2022	43
13. 24th August 2022	46
14. 25th August 2022	50
15. 26th August 2022	53
About The Author	57

Note For The Readers

Deepak Gupta asserts the moral right to be identified as the author of this book.

This book is almost a work of non-fiction and is based on a legitimate story. It's carefully designed to provide accurate and authoritative information in regard to the subject matter covered. The names, characters, and incidents portrayed in it aren't the product of the author's imagination but almost a real-life experience, still any resemblance to an actual person, living or dead, or events or localities are entirely coincidental. Our intentions are only to provide the accurate details of life events and we don't intent to hurt anyone's sentiments, feelings and thoughts. ***The advice and situations contained herein may not be suitable for everyone. You should consult with a professional when appropriate.*** Also, some real-life depicted scenes in this book may disturb you; thoughtfully discover it with a courageous heart. Consult with a competent professional when required.

Acknowledgement And Appreciation

We all know the world is extremely selfish, but good and kind people exist too. Plus, sometimes we have to be clever for our own good. You know, when you absolutely need some help, people would genuinely support you. They are worthy, just focus on how they spread their kindness than focusing on what wrongs they do to you. Appreciate their kindness because humans represent a mixture of both good and bad. Focus on positivity just like we all do in our lives. It was an exceptionally arduous journey to say goodbye to my mother and in between, many people and institutions aided us in many ways that made our journey easy. In the first place, I would like to thank, the **chief of IRCH, Dr. Sushma Bhatnagar**, for helping us to perceive the precise situation and guided us in the right direction. In addition, we would like appreciating **Dr. Ashish Sachan**, who helped us to diagnose the disease of my mother. Undoubtedly, he's extremely kind and much experienced in his field. We will always be indebted to him. Including all, we like to appreciate **AIIMS nurse Sudha ji** for making right efforts to guide and provide accurate information. Our family appreciate the wise people including **Sunil sir, Sanjeev sir, Sunny sir, Arun, Rajat, Chetan, Akansha, Varuni, Anjali, Avinash, Madhur, Diksha, Shubham, Lagan, and Anureet**. I would also like mentioning the name of most valuable asset of IRCH **Dr. Vashi**, Junior Resident, Pain and Palliative Care Unit. She's brilliant and kind while serving patients. She treated my mother with care and affection by which my mother always felt satisfied under her treatment. Her place was extremely significant in our journey. In the fullness of time, I would include the most prominent doctor who guided us psychologically and emotionally. Affirmative, a doctor of Max Hospital, **Dr. Megha Pruthi ma'am**, Pain and Palliative Care Unit. She has vast experience of dealing with end-care patients and family. With her guidance, our family were able to carry out the sensible decision and secured proper time to dedicate last goodbye to our mother. There are many names that can't be mentioned in this compact book, but they played a substantial role in our journey. They comforted us in humble ways that made our extensive journey simple. Finally, we appreciate the help and support of every kind soul in our family without whom I'm nothing. Remember, the journey was never a matter of money, but of the ideal time and company.

One day everyone will die, but it's terrifying when you know the exact time. The countdown to death will leave you in a dilemma whether to enjoy the remaining time & live in the illusion of life, or to interpret the process of death & leave the illusion of human life. When you know death is near, the best you can do is to forget it because it will come but life is deliberate. Every second, you have to push and appreciate everything in your life because day after day, now, you have to face extremely hard situations and you would forget the illusions of the situations which you conceived them as hard. The distressing situations aren't what we face in real life, but what we can't bear as humans, & when we are feeble to change creation and then look everywhere for some strange miracle. *Magic happens in fairy stories and when we think magic doesn't really exist. Our belief is magic, & because of that most magic happens.*

If you are reading this book, you have to be extremely strong because this will make you cry even when you don't want to. *This book will leave you in a dilemma of whether to love this book or hate the god.*

The book, ***The Untold Life of My Sage Mother*** *is written in tears and you will find stains on every page.* When we perceive pain in life, we should focus on strength and that's what life means to humans and is expected by God.

Prologue

I don't know how I should start this book because the pain would never allow me to weave the incredible story now. It's not the magical story of my mother. It's life itself, which is mostly untold.

Being a writer, I have been writing many books that include mental, physical and emotional costs. *Alright, most content seems fiction, but it's real.* Almost all writers write books based on their personal & real-life experiences. They convey most reality in books as fiction what they experienced. Even when you read the best-selling books, you will find many fictional stories so perfect that looks close to reality but my friend, every fiction once was writer's real-life perception & experience. Marvellous and fascinating stories look real because these steps were decided by God. *In reality, God exists as an invisible energy, that can wholly be felt in actions. That's why every move we take in our lives, looks perfect later and we say, thank God, we did this.* **Everything happens for a reason and most reasons come out very late.** Everything is planned, but it's God who decides what's the real conclusion of our planning.

I never thought I would have to write this book in a situation where controlling my own emotions would become a tough challenge for my soul. Indeed, I cried even while writing some fictional stories, but this is reality, life. I lived everything; every second, every moment, even while losing my emotional, physical and mental ability to accept the situation. It's true, I'm not mature enough to accumulate the entire story of my noble mother in a small book. **When my mother was dying, I promised her, I would write a book about how she transformed the whole life of** *our family. A mother invariably does a lot, even if the entire family can't return her debt for their whole life.* Just like, living is a process, death is also a process. Living and dying both require the persistent pain. It's bizarre, people live like they would never die and die like they never lived with us. It's just a feel, an energy which you can feel when they go, extremely far away from this world.

As a **family of five, including parents, two brothers and a sister**, we were extremely happy and satisfied with our lives. We struggled a lot to earn our everyday bread, and I think, everyone makes efforts to make their life better. It's extremely significant to know, when you commence your life from zero, you become fearless and courageous for life problems because you don't have anything to lose. Many people deceived us in our journey, but we never stopped doing good for others because that's what real humans are. *You can't stop doing good deeds just because people don't appreciate your goodness.* After struggling for years, we had made ourselves a good home where we could live peacefully. We were never towards greediness, but looking for what was necessary to experience life. **My mother taught, if you are gratified from the inside, you can grow from any stage of life. It's absolutely satisfactory, life is planned by humans but executed by God.** We all know, how we get anxious about matters like marriage, money, success, career, but these are merely bits of life. You can lose everything in your life, but if your loving people are with you, you can conquer everything. All achieve the destination; hardly a few enjoy the journey. Losing your own member is like losing half of your soul for a life. You can only crave for him forever. We can cry, feel feeble, beg, but nothing goes like we want because we don't control life; God does. *Have you ever seen the last moment how someone* *actually dies?* The moment is extremely painful to experience, and you will never be able to forget it for the whole life. Death is the silence in the face of a dying person. He just goes with the silent thought of expressing everything but unable to say anything. Just like there's process of life, there's a process of death too. No one dies just in a moment except the accidental deaths. Death comes with fear, but my mother faced everything bravely & silently, so that our family won't feel pain & fear with her. ***I'm not saying her sage just because she's my mother, but because she served a lot for our family where most people would run away.*** After experiencing, perceiving and reading many people, I can say, she was extremely selfless and kind even to donate everything including the entire resources of livelihood and wouldn't even feel regret in life. Many people deceived her because her character was like that. Good people are deceived by bad people.

Based on a true story, **The Untold Life of my Sage Mother** is focused on elaborating the unsaid tale of my mother's ways of living her passion and how she left life flawlessly. In her last time, our family members held her hand for the last three days where we could still feel her warm skin on our palms. ***When she was incapable to speak but able to listen, I promised her to write a book on her life which everyone would read and get inspired from her great life.*** I thought being too good doesn't exist, but after experiencing her the entire life, I understand, being extremely good exists but gets deceived by too bad people. She even remained selfless in her last time. ***I'm writing this book in tears because we lost someone who loved us like we born every day.***

When you lose your mother, the whole world becomes desolate. You will find her everywhere for the whole life.

With the pain, smile and strength given by her, you still live anyway.

ONE
17TH MAY 2022

Good people die very soon as God is looking for the best kind people who do the most righteous deeds in this mortal world.

With life, almost all have some life senses to live in this world, like being greedy, selfish, materialistic, but there are many people, too, who never cherish such things. These are selfless people and they can reshape the world into a world of love. When someone does unexpectedly good what most humans don't expect, the world can change and God is seeking such people. Being good with selfless motive, make you feel death in living life because they understand the real essence of life early, what most people learn with the facing situations and time. God takes away these people because it's the beginning of the end of Kalyug. Presently, a new world will begin with good people. *We know, there are many untold stories in which people die before someone knows about it, but trust me, telling the story of a mother needs a mountainous courage.* You can't write more about who gave you the birth of life.

Life isn't the coincidence of events, but the planned efforts of God. Every good we perceive isn't always good, and every

bad we perceive isn't always bad. Believe because that's life. Magic happens when we believe in its existence and strongly recognize the pure ultimate steps of God. God will not introduce his presence in reality, but he will come in the form of energy when you believe, just like you find god in immortal stones.

Okay, tell me, if someone feels a headache, do you feel he has a brain tumour? Absolutely no. Our Indian Medical Department has a system, and we follow that system in a good manner. On 17th May, my mother was on the terrace, taking a light walk. She was the only one in our home, who woke up before sunrise, mostly before 5 AM. She took a bath and went to the terrace garden as she always did. Absolutely, she had a mesmerizing beautiful terrace garden that look could impart you the feeling of entrance of the woods. Four years back, we bought our flat with an empty terrace and at that time, my brother and sister were managing jobs out of the station. So, when my father left for his work, my mother and I left in the whole house. As a writer, I always choose to work in a wide-open space, like in an open ground surrounded by greenery, a park or a terrace garden where I could feel the gentle wind that had passed through gorgeous flowers and herbs. While constructing the walls high, we have divided the sky and made our lives full of void spaces. Primitively, my mother was always curious to do something but had no hobby, so our family recommended her to grow some plants on the terrace. She was a modern person with open thinking but pure habits of a traditional rural type person, who loved to do desi things while connecting everything to nature. She always felt keen & delighted while preparing soil for plants, repotting them, growing new flowers, experimenting with new things and making food for earthworms. Our family accepts, our mind is conscious because of motherhood. She always took care of small creatures like she was listening to their voices. Every time she travels somewhere, she plucked some leaves, stems or flowers secretly and put them into a water bottle. *Almost entirely, she succeeded in growing everything she always wanted because she was curious to learn everything.*

I'm remembering, when she needed coco peat, manure, salts, pesticides, new plants or flower pots, she made delicious food and demanded us to bring these things. As she had already enough plants on the terrace, sometimes we felt irritated for asking many things, just like most people think. After our family, her passion was to take care of every plant like a mother does for her child. It was a deep connection. On the odd occasion, I also felt displeased when she woke me up at early morning and ordered me to bring the fresh cow dung because she needed that to make good quality soil at home. To make the soil fertile, earthworms are the best creatures and cow dung is their favourite food. Every time we travelled somewhere, she bought the seeds, plants, mature, or anything that could help her grow more plants. My mother was self-motivated by the output she was getting every day. **In total, she developed her passion along with household chores.** When our family actually needs our time, we go outside to earn our livelihood and get divided for the day. To make the house, a home, there's always a person mostly dedicated to home only. Caring for a home is a full-time job that most families neglect. Being an independent writer, I have been witnessing such situations very closely, how our mothers feel lonely at home and how, curiously, they wait for us for the whole long day and laugh with us like nothing had ever happened. ***A mother makes the house into a home of love. If anytime you get food when you reach home, say thanks to that dedicated person.***

Till that day, we were gratified & peaceful because our family was almost set. We had a home and good time. As we had grown from zero so we never got frightened of money, relatives, or anything. **We had developed the potential that could blow crucial problems with just a smile on our faces.** Like every day, she was on the terrace with my sister and we were asleep, like most young generations do these days. Every day she had the habit of plucking and eating something from her terrace garden like eating Tulsi, Neem, and fruit or Giloy to make herself healthy. She had fewer poor habits like most people have. She was always active and, on that day, she ate a Phoota, a home-grown fruit look alike a small melon. After eating it, she felt an extreme stomach ache, but after a few minutes, the pain went away just like a normal headache. As usual, stomach ache is a common problem, but we took it seriously and took her to a general physician, who thought maybe she had consumed something wrong. We were thinking casually & calmly, thinking of it as an ordinary problem. The doctor did some blood tests and thought it to be an infection, so she got the medicines. *There's a scientific fact; if you don't get healed with your medicines then you are eating the wrong medicines or maybe there are no medicines for your disease.* Time passed, May month ended and she had no relief. She didn't have the severe pain, but a mild pain that mostly went away on its own. On 31st May, our family was tense and after visiting the same family doctor, he referred us to Hedgewar hospital for further treatment.

In between 31st May and 9th June, X-ray and blood tests were done by doctors, and they were absolutely normal, but she still had the symptom of pain. She usually complained about how the pain moved every day from front to back and vice versa. As a result, on 9th June, her first ultrasound was done that depicted liver abscess and stones in her Gallbladder. We got less worried. Finally, the hospital doctors gave her the medicines for the liver abscess treatment and notified her to come later for gallstones treatment. We were glad because now we knew about the disease and medicines were given according to it. She was eating, walking, and drinking normally, but even with medicines, the pain wasn't going away. There was a sense of tension in the family. From 9th June to 21st June, she was on medication for **liver abscess** from Hedgewar Hospital doctors. With medicines there was no improvement, but the doctor recommended us to consume medicines for at least two weeks to recognize its effect, so we waited for it.

TWO
11TH & 12TH JUNE 2022

Do you believe in magic? What if God offered us the opportunity to feel everything before we die? I'm asking this question because everything our family faced was not just a coincidence but pre-planned steps by God.

I was always keen to grasp why God doesn't give us his real presence, but after looking back in our lives, I can assure you one thing, God is everywhere in what we are doing actually. He lies in the energy of our actions. Nothing moves without the decision of God. After COVID 19, our family started travelling to explore India. We visited many deep, mesmerizing, peaceful and ancient places of some states including **Gwalior, Jaipur, Agra, Mathura, Bhopal, Kurukshetra, Manali, Mussoorie, Khajuraho, Bharatpur, Mount Abu and at last Orchha.** You know, even at the age of 51 years, my mother retained the capability to walk 20 km a day without any discomfort. She constantly had a will to take a deep interest in the small things of life. She said, it's the minute things that God took most time to create, that's why the whole world is so lovely and meaningful. God gives attention to details to leave evidence of how small things can be created beautifully. Humans should pay attention to it to know what God had undoubtedly created.

We planned many trips and visited perfectly, but Orchha was the trip that astonished us at the end. On our trips, we explored the 1000 years old places, temples and caves and as always, we included temples in our trips, like Dilwara Temple in Mount Abu, Mathura Temples and the Orchha Raja Ram Temple. Originally, Orchha trip was created for 9th & 10th April, but due to heat waves, we tried to cancel. Everything happens for a reason; the homestay owner was too honest with his profession that he asked to shift our trip to later dates. Finally, we planned to go on 11th June. At that time, Orchha temperature was almost 45 degrees Celsius. You can travel nowhere in such a scenario. As my mother's health wasn't that good, she still got willing to join the trip. Basically, Orchha is a small town near Jhansi. It has some popular places like Orchha Fort, Betwa River, and Wildlife sanctuary. All the places are spread in the range of only 2 kms, and the rest is just woods. We planned to wander on feet, but after walking for around one km, she experienced unbearable pain in her stomach again. Our worries got inflated. The pain was so intense that she couldn't bear to walk even a single step. Due to this, we spent our entire day in the rooms of the homestay. The next day, she got better with the rest and was extremely happy and excited. Consequently, her willingness made us go to Raja Ram Temple. Orchha Town is commonly known as Raja Ram Ki Nagri. We worshiped there, and still after that, the pain rose in her stomach again. This was the last place she got to visit, and it was a temple. **You may call it coincidence, but that was the pre-planned steps of God because she mostly worshiped Lord Krishna and Lord Ram.** On our first trip, she visited Lord Krishna place, Mathura and Vrindavan and at last, Ram Nagri. Will you consider this as coincidence? She worshiped in many popular temples before dying. When the disease was gradually developing in her body, she had no symptoms and most doctors said, it took years to have any symptoms. So, when her death was already planned, she was travelling magically to worship every God of the most ancient places. God makes us believe by making us realise all his steps. We are astonished because we have never travelled much before except the last year. We travelled the most in our last year, and it was just because of my mother's destiny.

If you still don't believe in magic, the absolute tragedy of my mother's life will surely make you believe because everything was already planned, even nothing was revealed.

THREE
22ND JUNE 2022

As the general physician was our family doctor, we trusted him a lot. With the same ultrasound report, we went to him again in the hope of getting better medications, but again, he advised us to have an ultrasound to confirm the disease. Typically, ultrasounds don't reveal or elaborate on the whole disease. They only predict something, that needs to be confirmed with a CT Scan. On the second ultrasound report, the same liver abscess came again and he gave us the medicines again. After, every time we asked from mother, she always complained about persistent severe pain. With the new medications again, she made her way but got no relief. Lamentably, something came out that blew our minds at midnight. On 29th June, **Dark Red Rashes** started to appear on her whole body. We got extremely bothered because she never had any allergies for the whole life. In fact, at her 51 years of age, she had no sign of aging & never looked like a person of 51 years. The next day, those rashes became darker red. We rushed to the doctor, and he injected the medicine for allergy and infection. Just like a healthy person gets surprised when he gets some dangerous disease, our family were facing such a position.

When the treatment of any doctor doesn't cure the disease, what most doctors do, they refer and that's what our doctor did. On 3rd July, he referred us to **ILBS - Institute of Liver and Biliary Sciences** for better treatment. It was the time of morning when we called for the appointment of ILBS and got to know, the early appointment was for next month. In fact, we secured the appointment of 10th August, but it was too late. We had to deal with it as early as possible. After searching for best gastroenterology doctors in Delhi, we scrounged the internet and got the name of **Dr. Ashish Sachan, the best Gastroenterologist liver surgeon** whose Google reviews were almost 4.9 out of 5. This isn't a promotion, but I'm depicting everything with the right facts so, you get to know, good people still exist in this world.

FOUR
4TH JULY 2022

In India, most people lose their lives because they recognise their disease extremely late. Sometimes, it happens when we follow the wrong route.

Now a day, people are investing a lot of money on enhancing their houses but rarely spend money on their health. Most people perceive health check-ups as a money waste activity. The appropriate treatment can be provided if the disease is detected at the right time. On 4th July, we had the appointment of Dr. Ashish Sachan, Gastroenterologist, and Liver Surgeon in Dilshad garden. I, my brother and mother reached the clinic at sharp 6:30 evening for our first visit. My mother was still in pain, but except she was alright. As the doctor came, we were allowed to meet and explained everything with the reference of documents. You know, that night was the biggest nightmare of our lives. The doctor explained two possibilities; first may be my mother had the liver abscess, i.e. there may be some puss-filled mass on the liver and the liquid might get sucked out with a pipe. Secondly, maybe she had multiple tumours on the liver. Earlier, we didn't get it. He advised us to get a fresh ultrasound with the right centre, and he suggested

Sanjeevani Ultrasound Centre. We agreed. As soon as he said, we went to the centre at around 7 o clock, the same night. Coincidentally, my mother hadn't consumed anything for more than five hours as her eating habits had been reduced to extremes. Hence, it was the right time to get an ultrasound. In a few minutes, the ultrasound got done and we got the report. **The report was in technical terms, mentioned, some multiple lesions, and a difficult jumbled sentence with metastasis wording.** On that night, we still had time to revisit the doctor with that report, so, we rushed and showed the report to the doctor. Dr. Ashish Sachan is indeed very experienced in his field, and he read it in a few seconds, but before he could say something, he told my mother to wait outside. She went outside without a question. Our family has the best trust system and it's so strong that someone can ignore his gut feeling even if someone is uttering the lies. Most probably that doesn't happen, and that's why we trust each other blindly. My mother usually left everything on us, even the substantial responsibilities. She wasn't like a dominant person but a personality to give authority to people at a young age. Presently, my brother and I were still in front of the doctor.

'Maybe she has an advanced stage,' the doctor announced in a low voice. 'Now I can say something after a CT SCAN. Get her **CT SCAN** as soon as possible.'

We weren't much astonished as being advanced word was equivalent to us as a serious disease and not an incurable disease. As we got puzzled with that word, **ADVANCED**, we asked again, and he replied with the same answer, 'there may be a chance, she has an advanced stage. You should get her CT SCAN report as soon as possible.'

We went out with a questioning face and reached home. We were normally delighted like a family that got happy when they all meet. My brother is a curious man, and he had some doubts on why the doctor said advanced. He tried reading the report again with the help of Google, and even he sent the report to some good doctors and friends to get read by some experienced person. On the same night, I remembered clearly, he was on the terrace and called me when I was washing my face. As he called in the rush, I went with the moist face. He was crying. Yes, my brother had tears on his cheeks. I'm an optimistic man who always feels, there's a solution for everything and at night I was believing the same. In a moment, he announced, **'mummy has metastasis advanced cancer.'** Cancer, the word made me feel shivering in my entire body for a second. Metastatic means fast-spreading deadly cancer. Put differently, cancer cells are spreading rapidly in her body. I got everything.

'So, there's a cure,' I managed to ask a question with a pale face.

'No, there's no cure,' my brother replied in a trembled voice, while tears were already stained on his cheeks.

My eyes got moist with pain and fear. After a moment, my sister came and we revealed her everything. My father and mother were in the room, and we siblings were crying, trying to hide our faces. *We know she would die very soon, but how could someone accept this when their mother was still smiling and living absolutely well and the doctor said, there's no cure.* As our mother was still alive and active, we managed to suppress our tears and decided to not reveal her anything. We all decided we would do something and surely manage to save her. In total, we raised our motivation. With fake smiling faces with stains of tears, we entered the room. Our mother was absolutely fine and looking good. That night was the most interminable night of our lives, but it was just the beginning of the end. We were feeling a boundary of no trust in our family and in a dilemma whether to tell her everything or hide it. *What was the most challenging thing? To depict her that, you would die very soon and we can't do anything. No, we didn't have that courage to say something to our mother.* From that night, we were smiling with fake faces and every time we saw her, it was strenuous to hold back our tears. It was like, we had lost all our power in a night.

When someone in the family suffers from cancer, the whole family suffers from the same trauma of cancer, and everyone dies slowly, but in the end, not everyone would die. That day was the best day for my mother and family because a lot would happen that we never imagined in our whole life. You know, humans possess the unlimited potential to face anything. Our living family members are the evidence of this fact. **As a writer, we hype many of things, but the reading and life you will experience ahead, will forever change the way to look at your life. You will never be the same again after reading this book. Everyone is suffering, and that's why the world needs kindness. Our cruelty comes back to us in different ways. Be kind to the unkind even because we humans really need it the most.**

FIVE
5TH JULY 2022 - THE NEXT DAY

If someday you feel unhappy about your miserable moments in life, then remember the good days, smile, and face the pain because life is full of surprises. Sometimes the moment we believed of as bad, may become good when compared to the worst. Value the painful moments because that's life. It's not a part of life; it's life.

On 5th July, without any delay, we took our mother to **House of Diagnostics** near AIIMS. Sorry to interrupt you in between, but every day I accumulate too much energy and courage to write ahead. Frankly, I was doing procrastination of this book because every time I write, everything, every moment flashes in front of my eyes. My heart gets heavy, and I feel a sensation of sadness around happiness. My mother was alright at that time. In a few hours, the CT-SCAN got done. In **HOD**, I ache with some sadness in the air, like people were suffering from something that felt like their personal pain only. Generally, CT SCAN reports come in around 24 hours, but my mother's report came just after 15 minutes when the test was undertaken. HOD knew the significance of the report, and they handed the films, CD and a well explained report. In a few minutes, we took a cab to reach home. *My brother and I were reading the report and felt the report wasn't good.* We promptly sent the report to Dr. Ashish Sachan and our friends to know what was exactly written in the report. Straight away, the doctor advised us to meet personally so, we left mother at home and took our way to meet the doctor in the evening. The report was almost clear. We all three, including my father, were crying in the auto-rickshaw. It was practically impossible to control the tears when you knew, your mother would be dead soon and you could do nothing about it. **As we met the doctor, he explained, she had advanced Gallbladder Cancer that had spread to the liver and lymph nodes. It was a last stage advanced cancer that had no cure.** Our hearts were pounding, and a feeling of unconsciousness was eating us silently. The doctor elaborated on the best possible way to get the biopsy first and then a treatment plan to increase her life span. Before all else, it was extremely heart-breaking to accept that a simple stomach pain had now become the last stage of cancer overnight. How humans could accept this in one go. That day was the best stage of my mother's life, and we got stuck in confusion trying to do something. **Someone stated it right; you can't live life with the fear of death. Death is certain, but how someone dies, really matters a lot to the people who embrace them the most.** On that night, I posted a status on WhatsApp and Instagram to know if someone had any reference in AIIMS or not. The doctor suggested to us, *'You have to come out of shock because the status will not get changed. Focus on her treatment and she would live the rest of her life as best as she can.'*

What would you do, if you are stuck in the middle of the sea with a boat that has a big hole, of course you will try to cover it and that's what we attempted. On 7th July, we reached **Delhi State Cancer Hospital** and with the best possible way, we made the OPD card with the help of a security guard. Everything is a balance and just like, the world is a balance of good and bad people. ***A wise guard helped us to meet the doctor.***

The doctor explained, 'The cancer cells has spread to the liver and lymph nodes. It's already diffused in her blood. ***The positive sign in her case is, she has no symptoms of jaundice.'*** That was a good sign. Next, we got some medicines, no, no, not of any treatment but of stomach gas and pain. ***Every time someone has been diagnosed with cancer; the treatment is just chemotherapy, radiotherapy, and surgery (if it's not spread).*** We were satisfied as she got some medicines and a close check-up from the doctor. The day was looking successful, but with time, her pain was increasing. If you think this was the terrible time, then you would tremble to read ahead. ***No one dies easily. If you are witnessing the death of your loved ones, you would feel close to death even when you feel & stay alive. You will live with the realisation of a painful death.***

At night, we tried to admit our mother to AIIMS Delhi as an emergency case. A nurse assisted us that night. I have already said; wise people exist, and they help you to eternity. Always be kind to people. In an emergency, my mother's vitals like oxygen level, blood pressure of my mother got checked and everything was normal, except they said, she would die within six months. Her mortality was confirmed. *It's essential to know, our Indian hospitals work for success rate. They use hospitals resources for people who have better chances of survival than those who haven't.* Regrettably, we failed to get her admission, but everything happens for a reason. My mother was a kind personality who felt much livelier at home with family than being alone on a bed in a hospital. She was always optimistic in any situation and said, 'everything is normal. There's no need to get admitted. What would I do without all of you' but we knew everything. You know, it was extremely arduous to blink back those tears that were yelling to come out every day, even we could not cry in front of her. In AIIMS emergency, her UHID got registered and they referred us to IRCH – Dr. B.R.A Institute Rotary Cancer Hospital, AIIMS, a separate unit of AIIMS for cancer treatment but there was a long queue of people who were already waiting for their treatment. Every time I visited Hospital; I found people in deep silent pain, feeble and waiting for long for their turn to get treated, and we lost our senses even for our life careers. The man who has health, looks for other things, and the man who doesn't have it, leaves everything.

On 8th July, with some reference, we requested **Dr. Harsh Vardhan, Former Minister of Health and Family Welfare of India** to generate a letter for my mother's admission. My mother had a deep trust in AIIMS because her mother got also treated there successfully and lived till the age of 90 years. So, my mother had hope to get treated well. As we got the letter, my mother got delighted, like she was securing admission to a school. Now, she had to believe that she would absolutely get better. *In gist, she was a child soul with an intense curiosity in the little things of life. Everyone was happy because now she would get the treatment, but was there any treatment for her last stage of cancer?*

Between life and death, there's something that makes life, a happy moment and death, a sad moment. Something that

has no relevance when there would be no existence of any human in this world. One day, everything has to die and will be forgotten. Only life and death will stay; everything else will be forgotten. Forever.

On 9th July, after waiting for a few hours, she got admitted and met **Dr. Vashi**, a doctor from the north east who had an accent like that of someone who is playing a soft tune on a piano. She had a soft voice, a calm nature, and an attractive charm. My mother and brother both met the doctor and she diagnosed her for a few hours to identify everything about her life; past, what she did, what she ate, about ancestors. She asked every single thing about her life that could aid to find out something, and finally, she prepared a report. *That was undoubtedly a satisfying procedure. We were glad as it was the first time, someone was knowing about her disease in a comprehensive manner.* For some blood tests, they admitted the mother to a personal care unit and then discharged her later. In PCU, there were a few patients of last stages of cancer. Someone had a swollen belly while some patients were incapable to speak. It was almost a negative phase that could make you to the end of life. Until you have health, you have everything. If you have everything and not health, you have nothing. After some blood samples, they gave us the date of the biopsy when it was to be done. Almost it was also a successful day and her condition was better. Except pain, she was in a sound position. On 14th July, her biopsy got done, and we would get a biopsy report around two weeks later. *Under biopsy, the doctor takes a tissue of the tumour with the help of biopsy gun and it gets tested to know whether the tumour is cancerous or non-cancerous. In simple words, before they treat cancer patients, they prove the status of cancer in the body.*

In between the biopsy and its report, we talked to our friends, office mates and some knowledgeable people to see what could be done. Many suggested Ayurveda and told us, they have encountered certain cases where people have survived last stage cancer even in their last days. We got hopeful. My friend Avinash suggested an institution in Dehradun that could treat cancer patients with Ayurveda. We received many suggestions, but there was one thing, we could believe people who have experienced the situation personally.

Magic happens when you believe and become hopeful because that's how our body vibrates with energy and acts for what we believe and feel. Be hopeful and magic will happen. Non-believers don't believe in magic. They only think of good unexpected events as the coincidence of a deliberate life.

On 20th July, I was searching for filtered water cans because we felt there was something wrong with Delhi water because the most gallbladder cases were coming from Delhi. Unexpectedly, I reached a shop that was almost empty except for some water cans on the floor. He was around the age of eighty. His language and words were slow and sluggish. I asked for water cans, and he explained. I was feeling displeased because I was in a hurry, but he stopped me and asked, 'Why do you need water cans when there's good water supply. For whom do you need water?' I explained, 'I need it for my mother. My mother is a cancer patient.' He got shocked and asked, 'Which one?' I replied, paused, 'Gallbladder Cancer.' He told me to sit down, opened the drawer and brought out a small box that had some tiny irregular stones.

'My gallbladder got removed a year back; I had gallbladder cancer,' he announced with a lost face. I never thought, unexpectedly I could meet a man with the same cancer disease. I got curious and explained everything to him. He suggested to me two names of Ayurvedic medicines, **Kutki, and Chirayata**, some medicinal plants that could treat cancer. He also suggested me to go to Yamuna Nagar where we had to reach **Kaleshwar Mahadev Math Mandir in Kalesar**, **Haryana**, which gives Shiv Amrit & Ayurvedic Medicines to cancer patients. ***When you are feeble, even a small hope can give you immense strength.*** Without wasting any time, first, we went to Chandni Chowk market to buy those ayurvedic plants so that we could give them immediately. The next day, at 4 AM in the morning, I and my brother travelled to Yamuna Nagar to get Shiv Amrit. The Shiv Mandir is ancient, popular and exists in between the woods. There's nothing around it. The bus takes you from Yamuna Nagar and departs you in between the woods, just in front of Mandir. It's assuredly a mesmerizing and serene place where you can experience solely the peace. As, we were feeling like we had some progress, we were always glad with small achievements. In an hour, the Maharaj gave us medicines and said, ***'If there's some improvement in her condition, then this medicine will continue for a year.'*** As we got our medicines, we made our way to reach home as soon as possible. My mother had always a doubt because we were rushing and she was thinking, 'If there's only a small tumour, then why are they rushing?' She had some doubts, but as I repeatedly said, she trusted us blindly, and even sometimes she ignored her instincts for it. Around 11 o clock night, we reached home and my mother was still awoken. Slowly slowly her problem of insomnia was rising and sometimes she didn't sleep the whole night. As she was in bed for most time, it's normal for a patient to feel irritated. Finally, as we reached, we prepared a planning chart of how medicines would be given to her because there were already many medicines she was already consuming and everything was getting jumbled. So, we planned for her proper treatment. *Most time, our family felt highly motivated even for tough situations, so, we were extremely resolute for her treatment.* Now, at last, she was taking ayurvedic medicines for her treatment. It was the first time she was taking something for treatment. We were satisfied. **The biopsy report was still in the queue, and fingers were crossed for some hope.**

Moreover, we took her to a Dermatologist for skin rashes and a heart specialist for high blood pressure. Mostly, she had a high BP; maybe she had an instinct for something terrible. In gist, she was afraid somewhere silently. In a couple of days, her skin rashes went away and her BP got normal. So, there was some output for our efforts. ***That was good news, but after two weeks, the biopsy report came, and that devastated all the morale of our family. It was entirely the same as the CT SCAN report, depicting a Malignant Cancer. All our hopes flew away in a moment.***

SIX

1st August 2022

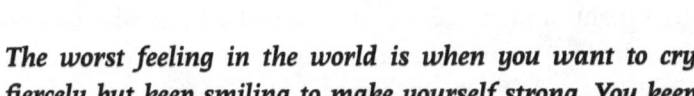

The worst feeling in the world is when you want to cry fiercely but keep smiling to make yourself strong. You keep smiling and tears get dead inside, making a grave of feelings to be locked forever.

When a person dies, he doesn't know he would die until he gets extremely close to death. August remained a terrible month for our family. My mother experienced the first symptoms of jaundice and yes, that was the beginning of the end. **When cancer spreads to the liver, the symptoms of jaundice appear.** This wasn't ordinary jaundice. **According to reports**, her gallbladder had collapsed and there was a tumour lying in her stomach that was the size of almost a cricket ball. Her bile duct got blocked, so it wasn't supplying any bile juice for the digestion of food. When the liver stops functioning, someone can't even digest the medicines and water. From 26th July, she had slight symptoms of jaundice that was hardly appearing in her eyes and nails. We live in a flat that could hardly occupy five people. My brother and sister are teachers and they get limited holidays. My father is a tax consultant who has to meet certain deadlines. *Most time, I got isolated with my mother. I tried making her feel*

entertained with new topics, jokes, TV and encouraged her for the treatment, but we all knew the result. From August, she had left eating the food and her body was completely on juices. She was drinking three juice glasses a day. We even made her eat, but she was incapable to swallow with her whole heart. Every time she ate something; she vomited. Pain and vomiting were spoiling the quality of her last days. She mostly vomited 5-6 times a day & sometimes even more. She required 24 hours full day care and our family was extremely stressful to see her like that; pale and weak.

When you have no option, you go anywhere. For the treatment of jaundice, we approached a baba who treated jaundice with some jhada. I know, this was an extremely foolish step, but when someone is gradually dying is front of you, sometimes you believe the things that you don't even think about. *All was useless. Nothing changed.* Moreover, we made some ayurvedic kada for her jaundice treatment. There was slight improvement but no treatment. I remembered, how I took my mother in an auto-rickshaw and she laid her head on my shoulder. It's extremely unfortunate to bear the head of a mother who could die anytime. ***The mother who always took care of us, was suffering from something that couldn't be reversed. She had a great will and never cried even in extreme pain. You can find another woman but can't find another mother.*** When someone suffers from cancer, whether it's first or last stage, both patients suffer equally. The mental trauma of having cancer is unbearable. **The days passed and we had to wait. How difficult was to wait for someone's death. Those were the scariest days that I couldn't even elaborate in words.** With time, her capability to drink juices was reducing. Now she could drink nothing half a glass. *With that slow trauma, we were mentally, physically and emotionally drained.*

Due to medicines, most time, she felt sleepy and lost interest in the things she loved except her plants. Even in unconsciousness, she informed us to water the plants properly. Plus, even after taking the sleeping pills, she was mostly awakened all night. We were helpless, so we decided to stay awake with her, so she could feel pleasant. I remembered how she complained that she was unable to sleep because her mind was working extremely fast. Her mind was not calm as a normal human being. **The cancer cells had already reached her brain, and she was acting strangely hour after hour.** You know, a cancer patient experiences exponential degradation. *One day you could find him eating and the next day, they wouldn't be able to swallow the food and another following day, difficulty in drinking water. It was terribly challenging to prepare our minds for such an exponential downfall.*

As time passed, her pain increased. It was so intense that she started to cry even with painkillers. She was eating four to five painkillers a day that equally had extreme side-effects. Someday she was totally awakened while someday too sleepy. There was no balance in her life. Like, she was getting close to death; likewise, we were going also. The only thing that we survived was one step just before death. As her changes were too quick & drastic, our whole family started to sleep in the same room, so that we could hear and monitor her easily. In everything, my sister managed her job and household work very well that made mother's treatment simple. She had done a lot of work to make our family. Every time we went to the hospital; she made the food, cleaned the house, washed our clothes, and even took close care of the mother.

In August, many incidents happened that required extreme deep details. Everything was rough, and my mother was still complaining of her stomach pain. Her pain generally moved around her stomach that made her scream for medicines. At last, AIIMS Doctor said, now there's no treatment for her cancer. We were feeble to reveal her the truth, so we told her that we got a new date of two weeks later. While suppressing everything, we were living life like there was a thin line between mother and rest of the family. We bought so many ayurvedic medicines in the hope of her treatment. Even we took a medicine of **ATS**, Saheb, who is popularly known as the **Passenger of God**. The Saheb medicine was extremely effective, and she was gaining some energy by consuming it. *She had a lot of faith in God and every time she asked for something from God, it was directly from her generous heart.* We had already managed to pass a month without crying. It was like, we were restraining tons of tears in our eyes.

On 12th August, her symptoms became more visible. I remember, there was Raksha Bandhan on that day. We did all the rituals early with no enthusiasm. Every time our mother asked for something, we bought it without any thinking. When she was feeling pain, we purchased every type of massager, at least that could reduce her pain. **We had money in our hands but weren't able to spend even a single penny on her treatment. If there was a treatment, she could be treated even without money.** It's burdensome when we want to hug our loved ones and still can't because we haven't revealed she was living her last days.

As our family hadn't experienced someone's cancer except the cancer of my cousin who died just after his marriage. He was diagnosed with the intestine or colon cancer in the second stage, so it could be cured. He was treated at Rajiv Gandhi Cancer Institute. He received a couple of chemotherapy and also got treated well, but after six months of treatment, his tumour came back and he died because chemotherapy got wrongly reacted in his body. When he died, his body was five times bigger than that of his actual body, and then we knew, chemotherapy isn't simple as it looks. As my mother was diagnosed with cancer, everyone was saying, there will be chemotherapy, but our family was afraid because our experience with it wasn't that pleasant. Some were saying, you shouldn't go for chemotherapy, it's risky and that would deteriorate the current quality of her life. We were waiting for the fake doctor's date, and the dilemma was consuming us every moment.

SEVEN

14TH AUGUST 2022

Do you believe life provides chances to us when we do something wrong? Indeed, life gives us the opportunity to change that really needs to be changed.

On 14th August, my mother's condition was extremely terrible. Her entire body was heating badly, including her stomach, which had become enlarged, bloated, and heated like a tandoor. As she was on palliative care, we had to do everything we could do to comfort her symptoms. It was like feeling her sharp pain, getting emotionally drained in between, and then preparing back again to comfort her even with the stained face. **We thought every day as the worst, but a cancer family faces the most unfortunate days after every day. By all means, every day was her best and worst day, best because the situations would get much worse later, and worst because her condition was deteriorating every hour, which was entirely unexpected.** The tumour inside her stomach got hotter every day. We typically gave her juices and did cold & hot therapy after every few hours. Even with therapy, her symptoms weren't getting relief, and she already knew that her time had come. She was in intense pain that she could never experience during her entire life.

At night, her symptoms got worse, and she started to weep shrilly that could tear anyone's heart in a moment. That was the harshest time of our lives. She had a gut feeling that her time was near. The time was around 3 AM at night and most time, we didn't know when we got awake and when we actually slept because there was no schedule. **On that night, she cuddled me, my brother and sister, and said, 'My time has come. Promise me; you all will get married and always be together. Never fight with each other, whatever the situation is.'** We all were crying because we knew what could happen next but that night was the most crucial opportunity of our lives. Somehow, her will and God's miracle helped her to survive. I already said, she had the greatest and strongest will I had ever seen. As we didn't tell her about the disease, she even killed her own instinct because she trusted us. She wanted to live and attend the marriage of my sister. *She had only one dream and for which we were wandering and exploring families to get our sister married but someone said it right, even after you fulfil many of your dreams, you would still feel like something is still incomplete, because that's how life is planned, complete, yet incomplete.*

That night God gave us one more opportunity to reveal her the entire truth. Why it was so significant to reveal her the truth. Should someone reveal about her approaching death? But death will still come, no matter what.

EIGHT
15TH & 16TH AUGUST 2022

When you think everything is random in life, then perceive the conclusion, look back, observe, absorb, and understand that everything was planned. Everything is definitely planned. Every move is pre-decided.

15th and 16th August were the days that she was struggling to drink even half a glass of juice. Chiefly, she was drinking only one quality of juice, pomegranate, because that was giving her more energy. From the last month, she had moved from a healthy person to a patient of critical condition. **The phase was unimaginable. Someone can be happy with less money, but no one can be satisfied with less health.** Every day we visited a cancer patient dietician to find out what she could take in her diet. Sometimes she drank chicken soup, vegetables soup, or oats, but as time passed, she found chewing food as like the most arduous task of her life. She almost left eating food and was only on juices. We tried making her eat, but she vomited. We all know, protein is the vital intake for the human body and without it, you would feel less energy in your body. Seeing her degrading condition, we decided to contact a doctor who could assist us on how to comfort the end-life of a cancer patient. We had accepted the fact that she was living her last days, but we were undertaking everything that we could do; conceivably we were expecting some miracle. Very well, we were waiting for a miracle. In the hope, we decided to meet **Dr. Megha Pruthi ma'am**, a **Pain and Palliative care** doctor at Max Hospital. We took the appointment and got a chance to meet her. She's extremely serene, gentle and a person who wants to explore the roots of patients and then give the satisfactory treatment to it. In gist, she knows what she actually does. She's not only a qualified doctor but also a good psychologist who knows how to comfort and guide the family in the appropriate direction.

As my mother was unfit to come, she sent a short video through my mobile, but the doctor decided to make a video call to her to know her current condition. She talked to her for about ten minutes to find out about her concrete condition and the doctor said, 'She's active and looks good.' My mother only complained about her pain that was moving from the stomach to back. The doctor noted everything in detail and made the right prescription. In between the talks, we told the doctor, we haven't revealed the truth about her disease. The doctor ma'am was in astonishment and said, I think, 'You have already taken her to cancer hospital. She's educated, so even if you haven't revealed, maybe, she knows everything. Every person knows what's going inside his body, so she also knows even if you say nothing about it. Moreover, you should tell the truth about her disease because it may hamper your family trust. I have witnessed cases where in the last moment of death, the patient blames the family for not revealing the entire truth. It is possible she has some dreams, last desire, want to meet someone or anything. You should tell her because your case is critical. She will die anytime, so it's better, you tell her everything. Seize the moment and tell her everything. Death will come whether you tell her the truth or not. **Nothing will change with your truth, but it will help her realise her last time. Today is her best day.** Maybe she can utilise her somewhere. Don't give her fake hope. She has hope that she will become well, but the reality is different. Understand, when you get the moment, tell her. It's my suggestion and the rest are all up to your family.'

We also knew, the doctor was telling the truth because by hiding the truth, we were also feeling like culprits. A thin wall of hiding emotions was eating us deeply, and we also wanted to reveal it as soon as possible. Dr. Megha Pruthi ma'am gave us the right direction to tell the truth. At least we would share what we wanted to. ***Don't you think, on 14th August night, God gave us the opportunity to reveal the truth?*** I told you, everything is planned. All you have to do is, trust the process and you will look back and smile because you can't change what has already happened.

NINE

17TH AUGUST 2022

When her cancer was detected, she continuously encountered the problem of staying awake all night. The severe pain, cancer cells and tumours made her body in a non-resting position. It was so difficult that every time she tried sleeping, the pain appeared. When we met Dr. Megha Pruthi ma'am, we told her about my mother's insomnia. She said, 'There are no close to perfect medicines to comfort the symptoms of cancer patients.' The normal mg power medicines weren't working on her body. The doctor changed the medicines to some intense power, so that my mother could sleep. She also had the problem of vomiting that was degrading her life experience every day. I remember, after taking the medicines, she slept continuously for two days. Every time we tried waking her up, she asked, 'Why are you disturbing me?' By waking her up, we gave her the medicines and juices. **The balance was lost in her life.** Sometimes she stayed awake and alert for a couple of nights and sometimes she stayed sleeping for days. Accordingly, the medicines actually blocked the nerves that send signals to the brain, and that's why she felt drowsy most of the time. Her symptoms got relieved, but she was sleeping all the time. On 17th August, she woke up after accumulating all her strength and went to take a bath. We were waiting for that opportunity for a long time because we didn't know what would happen the next minute.

As my mother came into the room, we all were already there. My father and I were on the three-seater sofa while my sister, brother and mother were on a double bed. We took a moment and had already decided that the senior brother would reveal her the entire truth.

'Mummy,' my brother said in a depressed tone. 'Is everything all right?' He asked mother.

'Yes beta,' she replied with less enthusiasm.

My brother got hesitated while looking at everyone's faces and we were elevating our eyebrows at him to tell her everything. He blinked positively.

'Mummy, the doctors have no cure for your disease,' my brother announced while controlling the copious tears.

'No cure, means?' My mother got surprised, but it was less than we expected.

My brother announced again, 'Doctors have no treatment for your disease but don't worry, these days they haven't even any cure for a headache or jaundice, he said sarcastically. We even added to make his point stronger.

'But Ayurveda can treat you,' I added. 'That's why we went to buy ayurvedic medicines. Don't worry mummy. These doctors don't have cures for most diseases. Don't worry.' We were comforting our own opinions but as we were restraining our tears for a long time, everyone burst out with plenty of big tears that paused for a second. My mother got emotional and hugged everyone into her arms and said, *'I will not die till the age of 90. You all will get married in front of me. I'm not going anywhere.'*

She wiped everyone's eyes, but we continued crying because we knew what was the factual reality. My mother had deep faith in Ayurveda and that's why she believed she would get a cure for sure. **As I already said, she was a very optimistic person who could give you motivation even if she knew about her own death.** We knew the deep discussion of doctors, but she knew truth only from our side, even as a positive side. She was damn sure to get the treatment and of course, why she couldn't believe it as she was still well on 17th August. That was the day, when we really cried in front of her. We even told her that she could share anything she wanted, even how uncomfortable the situation was. After we told her the truth, we were feeling extremely light and felt like faith and trust had been restored. At least, now she knew what was actually going in her body. We even asked about her wishes, may be if she wanted to meet someone, or go somewhere, doing something, but she resisted all and said, 'I'm not going anywhere. You will see.' *Today, I feel that moment and understand; she knew everything but she didn't reveal her noble emotions. By smiling in front of us, she was keeping the profound moment intact in our family.*

I still have the instinct that my mother knew everything, but she didn't share because she knew her family would get shattered. She gulped every pure emotion, made them dead, and kept smiling to remember her smiling face, not her crying sad face.

Losing money is nothing; a ruined career is nothing; no home is nothing, and losing is nothing. Care for the energy and people because that's for we are in life. Losing someone is like experiencing someone dying inside an alive body.

TEN

19th August 2022- Janmashtami

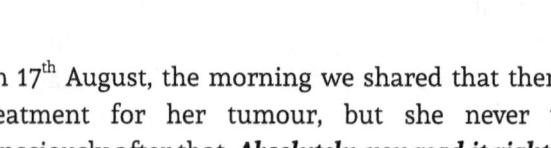

On 17th August, the morning we shared that there was no treatment for her tumour, but she never woke up consciously after that. **Absolutely, you read it right.** Jaundice had reached her brain and was creating a kind of confusion in her mind. We had a table lamp in our main room whose golden light had seen the laughter and enjoyment of our family, but now that light was witnessing the toughest phase of our lives. Literally, I was starting to hate that light. My whole family was feeling insecure and terrified for small incidents because death could capture my mother at any moment & we didn't know what was her last moment. Consequently, we wanted to be around during her last time, but its true, death doesn't come instantly; there's a process of everything.

On 19th August, when everyone was celebrating the Janmashtami festival, we were in severe pain because my mother was sleeping continuously for days. *It was the first time; she kept sleeping for days in such an auspicious kind of festival. She was a child that always felt the most excitement on festivals, even we kept doing things after asking her everything.* Observing the family situation, we decided to keep the festival simple. I remember, my sister had prepared everything and our whole family was remembering how the last year we celebrated the Janmashtami Festival with great enthusiasm, pomp and show. My mother always had the passion for listening to the songs of the 70s, 80s, and 90s. Also, she loved listening to devotional songs including her favourite song, **Kanhaiya Le Chal Parli Paar**, and on that day, the same song was playing on TV. I laid my heavy head on the left hand of my mother because she wasn't responding consciously & clearly. As the song was playing, the tears rolled down my cheeks and I felt like drowning into the deep sadness. We were distressed because my mother wasn't moving to worship the Lord Krishna for which she was always ready, no matter whatever the situation was. But suddenly, my mother woke up; yes, she had felt tears in my eyes. First, she wiped my tears and said, **'Deepak is getting emotional with the song. Don't worry, I'm not going anywhere.'** At that moment, she accumulated all her strength to worship Lord Krishna. She sat on the bed in another room and chanted a mantra like we all subconsciously do. She was chanting mantras extremely fast, like she was in a hurry. I had seen how she was controlling her sleep. That day, she woke up for our family to worship Lord Krishna. You will be astonished to know; Lord Ram and Lord Krishna were both her first and last worship simultaneously. *We thought of her sleeping as the worst experience, but the days we would perceive of her life, almost drained our family entirely. That day was* *officially the beginning of the end by God. Even when she was sleeping, those were her best days because after that, the days we faced, were the gloomiest days of our lives, or maybe they always will be.*

ELEVEN

20TH – 22TH AUGUST 2022

Recently when I was writing this book, I heard an actor named **Rahul Koli** unfortunately passed away due to cancer at the age of 10. Just after his breakfast, he vomited blood thrice, got multiple fever, and died after. He was suffering from **Leukemia**, mainly a blood cancer disease that kills the immunity of a person. Put differently, it's a cancer of blood-forming tissues, hindering the body's ability to fight infection. His only film titled, **The Last Movie**, came to Oscar and just before its release, he died. That's how deadly cancer is. I remember the time when we heard about cancer rarely. It was a rare disease, but now it's common or maybe we are too aware of everything. **When someone is diagnosed with cancer, he may live one day or 10 years & it's hard to find out.** When my mother was diagnosed with cancer, AIIMS Delhi issued us the statement that she would die within six months and we thought, six months less. Also, I heard about the story of a little girl who was diagnosed with cancer, and doctors said she would die within a week, but now the magic is, she's still alive and living a healthy life. She's even marrying her son's child. **Alright, life is unpredictable.**

From 20-22th August, my mother's condition got worse than expected. One day she was walking on his feet and the next day, her feet trembled. We were not even ready to absorb such brutal shocks. I remember the day, when we met Doctor Atul Sharma, the most competent doctor in North India. You may find his information on the internet very easily. Waiting from early morning to evening, we got the opportunity to talk to him for only two minutes, and he said, 'There's nothing in your case. Chemotherapy will do nothing. You are extremely late.' I barely met with the doctor because my mother was all alone on the first floor on a mat, waiting for some hopeful answer. **During the whole day, she talked to a boy of around 15 years who had been coming to AIIMS since the age of two.** Yes, he was diagnosed with a brain tumour at the age of two. My mother was a very kind and emotional person. As the boy was looking poor, unfortunate and feeble, she talked and gave him a seat near her. On the same day, when we returned home, we convinced our mother that the doctor was extremely intelligent and he had written us a medicine but it could harm your health, so we would see whether we should give it to you or not. She even told us about the brain tumour boy and said, 'People are suffering much in their lives. At least I have a problem that has some solution or treatment.' *Literally, she never expected she would get diagnosed with an incurable disease.*

As our days were similar to nights, we weren't sleeping much because now our mother was getting trouble even to stand on her own feet. Due to her excessive weight, she was unable to control her body. She always needed someone who would take her to the washroom and even go inside because she was feeling some sort of confusion. Sometimes she kept pulling the toilet paper continuously or washing hands continuously, even when we turned off the tap. The confusion in her mind had started. Sometimes her mind got stuck on the same activity again and again. She troubled, thinking clearly and saying anything clearly. On the same night, we were extremely exhausted as our physical condition was compounding every day to become worse. We were tired, but we couldn't sleep or rest as a normal person does. Even when we slept, we mostly felt insecure, which was eating us mentally and emotionally. Bizarrely, in the middle of the night, my mother woke up for the toilet. My sister also woke up to take her to the washroom. We would always be indebted to our sister because we couldn't imagine the mother's care without her. She was the only one who could do a few essential things.

As I said, my mother felt confusion, so while returning from the toilet, she suddenly walked towards another room in a hurry, and I, and my brother were sleeping on the floor. In confusion she fell on us in a microsecond, and it was absolutely fortunate that my brother saved her head from getting injured. She yelled in confusion. Sometimes she yelled at us, but that was her mind's confusion or reflex action. We know, she had no bad feelings in her heart. After, she fell on the floor and my blood pressure dropped. I almost had a mini heart attack, and it took me a few seconds to get conscious to know what exactly had happened. It was the most horrible night of our lives. She was on the floor and even after accumulating all the power, we couldn't be able to put her on the bed. In some way, we had to place her on the bed. We can't leave her on the cold floor. We knew, her legs were almost dead and we all were trying to grab her from her shoulders, but her legs were motionless. She couldn't transfer energy to her legs. After an hour of doing odd efforts, we put her on a strong floor mattress and then put her on the bed. **After that night, I was always seeing the pale face of my mother because the insecurity had risen in our minds. I was unable to sleep because we didn't know what would happen next.** Her symptoms were changing more rapidly than we were absorbing the shocks. I vomited a lot that day because my digestive system got unbalanced due to a negative chemical reaction that happened in my body. *I was feeling uneasy even of slight noises. Cancer kills people many times before the real patient dies.*

From that night, we knew one thing; she would die, but death doesn't come easily. A cancer patient faces what a healthy human can't imagine for the whole life. It's a deep, unbearable pain and experience that can't be felt without touching it.

TWELVE

23RD AUGUST 2022

Till the morning of 23rd August, we were recovering from the last dreadful night that didn't come with sleep but with the horrible life experience. When we met Dr. Megha Pruthi ma'am, she explained, **a jaundice cancer patient generally dies in a week or two but my mother had crossed three weeks with the symptoms of jaundice, and that was both good and bad news;** good because maybe our ayurvedic medicines had some positive impact on her health, and bad because maybe she would show some unexpected symptoms later. From that morning, she had too much confusion, repetitions, hallucinations, and even a problem with remembering our names. Bedridden for almost two and a half months, she wasn't feeling well while resting all the time and not even good while sitting. She wanted to walk, but her legs weren't moving as she wanted. Overall, she had no peace and was struggling every moment. From that day, she repeatedly told family members to make her sit and after a second, told us to lay her on the bed. Maybe it was her reflex action to the pain but she called us to this lay-up and sitting position almost 500 times a day. She was repeatedly saying the same thing. It was tiring for our family members to see her like this. She mostly said, **Uthao, Bithao, Uthao, Bithao,** and so on. Also, sometimes we didn't make her sit and said, **'Utha Diya Aapko,'** and she said, okay. It meant, she had confusion in her mind; even her impulses weren't in proper control.

The day disappeared with such unbearable incidents. Sometimes we massaged her feet, applied Multani soil, did hot and cold therapy and anything that could keep her cool, peaceful & painless. She slept all day and every time we woke her up for food, she left all her body weight to ourselves. She had entirely lost control all over the body. Every time we looked at her sleeping face, we found it as the same as the face of a deceased person. The glow of an alive person had vanished from his face. *Mostly, her eye lids were half-open; her mouth was partially open, like you couldn't recognise whether she was sleeping or not.* Most time, we tried to talk to her and asked, 'Pyaari mummy aap sun Rahe ho' and she just said, haan in a very deep slow voice and nothing else. **Can you imagine, how we were able to control our emotions.** Some other days, she saw ourselves without blinking her eyes for seconds, and we got frightened, like maybe someone had seized her soul. The night came and that was much unexpected. As we already said, she was sleeping most time and during that time, we were holding her hand, one by one, to keep her aware of our presence. Suddenly, in the middle of the night, she started crying after waking up from horrible dreams in which she was seeing her dead ancestors and said, 'Someone is making me tired. Someone is calling me. I need to go.' It was an extremely unpleasant situation and also a horrible situation that was trembling her legs. She was acting like a child. To comfort her, we hugged and patted her back and said, 'It was all dream. Nothing is happening. No one is calling.' My brother and I were researching a lot on the internet about how someone die and what are the signs of someone who is near death, and we found something strange; first, by symptoms of hallucinations and confusion, and second, by seeing their dead ancestors or close loved ones. We already had the indication that her end was near, but the end has no time. It can come at any time. At that night, we also read Hanuman Chalisa to keep her positive and stay away from these energies but if we saw this phenomenon from scientific side, it was all her confusion, like sometimes she called a name Vibhuti, a character from Bhabhi ji Ghar Par Hai Serial, and said, he wanted to kill her. *It was clear she had random thoughts & confusion, but experiencing it with our own mother was extremely painful to see. We never imagined her like that. After, we all slept for an hour, woke up, and slept again to give company to our mother.*

It's painless to see cancer as simple, but those who experience it become tough for a lifetime. It's a lifetime troublesome situation to overcome and comforts our minds to forget all the minute details someone has experienced clearly.

THIRTEEN
24TH AUGUST 2022

When everyone goes for their work, it's only the mother that works for the whole family for the whole life with a smile on her face and no complaints in her heart.

The doctors had already confirmed that my mother could die anytime, and it might be next minute, hour, week or month. It's indeed difficult, tough, and bizarre, like we were waiting for her death to free her from every pain. Sometimes we also had some conflicts in these situations. On 24th August morning, my mother had a very critical condition. We tried to wake her up, but her body wasn't in control. We all three tried to make her sit and tried to give her a liquid ayurvedic medicine, but she was unable to swallow even one tablespoon. I read somewhere, people who are close to death, leave the food, and even drink a glass of water. It was scary because our minds were already afraid and burning with these thoughts. In fact, we couldn't make her drink one drop after a few minutes, might be, it could choke her throat. Her body wasn't responding properly to our signals. After trying our best, we allowed her to lay on the bed, and she stayed asleep all the time. The medicines were of such an intense power that she wasn't able to feel anything in her body. ***If she could feel her body, she could feel pain, too. To comfort her, we had to sacrifice control of her body.*** From the last two months, we were only swallowing food just to keep ourselves alive. We were tired at every level, so finally, somewhere in latent form, we accepted that her end was near. Finally, we decided to have some attendants in the home that could help us in taking care of our mother. Mainly, the idea of attendants was given by Dr. Megha Pruthi ma'am, because she said, in such tough situations, many people even leave their work, jobs and regret later. *My mother needed 24-hour care, so we decided to have two, 12-hour attendants that would help us in taking care of mother and in that meantime, we could do work, household chores, decision making, and accomplishing anything significant.*

The same day, she was unable to eat or drink anything, even the medicines she usually took. So, we thought, a **Ryle tube** – a narrow food tube passed into the stomach via the nose and at least she could get the necessary food to keep her energetic. After a lot of efforts, we got a team of nurses that came at around four in the evening. They gave us a few significant instructions, got signed some papers and finally installed Ryle and urinal tubes. Even my mother hadn't eaten anything; her stomach was much bloated than usual. As they inserted the Ryle tube, a red coloured concentrated fluid came out. It was reverse fluid from the pipe and almost a mug got filled. The nurses informed, **'Her last day liquid is still intact. Her digestive system isn't working.'** We got the point, absolutely, the nurses were talking about her liver. I have heard from many people, when the liver stops working, someone can't even digest the water. Therefore, everything was crystal clear. Also, the urinal tube was inserted properly with some unnecessary mess that could be avoided. Now, my mother was like a baby; even my sister made my mother to wear an adult diaper. In total, she wasn't able to do anything on her own. The evening ended with some preparations. Sometimes my mother had reflexes when she found some stranger in her room. Immediately, she called my name and sister's name unconsciously. So, it was clear, she couldn't express, but with a less conscious mind, she was understanding everything. In closing, at night, my mother got her medicines in the form of liquid from Ryle tube, and we took relaxed breaths. **Everything got neat & clean in her room and more organized than before.** The first attendant came at around 8 PM to work till morning 8 AM and the next attendant would join. We had an attendant's seat on a three-seater sofa, and my mother was still sleeping next to my sister. The others were sleeping in another room. Also, the attendant checked her vitals and informed, 'Her oxygen level is fluctuating very rapidly, we should keep a small oxygen can for the case of emergency.' We did as she said. Finally, we all laid our heads on the pillow. Earlier, we mostly had anxiety, and a sense of insecurity about what would happen if we all slept, but now a proper trained attendant was tracking her health and that was a good sign for her caring. Have you noticed that my mother was sleeping for so many days, and that was a clear sign of her near death? **In gist, the day started with a mess, but ended in some organized way.**

When someone is feeble, pale and extremely down, he wants hope, the magic to happen, believing in the superstitions, trusting the unbelievable, waiting for miracles and understanding the gods. **God is energy and his** *presence in our lives is vibes and energy. His magic works when we believe, because that's how we put our efforts into our belief. So, that's why the human itself is responsible for everything and don't blame God when you don't believe in him. Believe the divine energy around yourself and you can steal what most people would never be able to believe.*

FOURTEEN
25TH AUGUST 2022

Hope isn't really a terrible thing. When doctors told us, there's no treatment for our mother. We still made our hope and did everything we could do, so that we wouldn't feel guilty for not trying our best. Not every time hope works, but hope is the way to reach the destinations whose journeys are difficult.

The next day, 25th August, we all woke up, at least our eyes weren't heavy, but everything had already become more terrible in the morning. My mother was snatching deep breaths and every time we were trying to look at her, she looked almost equivalent to dead. Yes, I know what I'm stating. The only thing we could feel was just heavy breaths. We were trying to encourage her and asking, whether she's listening to us or not. She mostly replied only with a gaping mouth, with a deep breath, like she was accumulating all her strength to talk to us. We all were holding her hands and thought her end was near. This was really a painful moment. The last night, when the attendant tried to give her juice and medicines, liquid came out of Ryle tube. The attendant said in pain, 'She's not digesting any liquids.'

Even my mother's urine output was just 200ml and extremely thick. They said it was abnormal. After a lot of discussion with family, we decided to remove the Ryle tube and urinal tube because it wasn't contributing her anything but increasing her pain. The next attendant had arrived, and the last one had to leave. We were confused & in a dilemma because her condition was almost equivalent to dead. While controlling our emotions, we talked in AIIMS emergency and they said, 'You can bring her in emergency. Her vitals are abnormal.' Finally, we decided to talk to Dr. Megha Pruthi ma'am, and she told us, 'It's time to be with your mother. You can take her to hospital, but it's like increasing a few more days to get her more suffering.' We had to get familiar with the reality that she could go anytime; and rushing and hustling to take her anywhere wouldn't solve anything. We also thought, how could she be on a ventilator because she was suffering from malignant cancer and not with some accident or organ failure. If we took her to hospital, her suffering would increase. **Doctor explained, 'Now she will not be able to tell you about her pain. You can feel her closed fist or some stress on her head while she's suffering from pain. Now, she will not be able to speak, but she will listen to everything. In her end time, praise and appreciate her values; and her contribution in your family and the world.'** Dr. Ma'am's words made our whole family in tears, and we decided to make every attendant leave. After some documentation, both attendants left and Dr Ma'am suggested giving her medicines through her veins. I rushed to buy medicines and found a good doctor. That day, my mother's main problem was fever and severe pain. Doctor ma'am said, 'You will feel like she needs food but in reality, she doesn't. Don't worry. Be with her in her last time.'

It's scary to find a certain time between life and death. It's better when we have a little uncertainty of everything.

The doctor came, and he injected the doses for both pain and fever. *That was a relief because at least now, she wasn't in pain and her temperature got normal.* In the evening, the doctor gave her another dose for the same and decided to come tomorrow for the same doses. We all were crying like hell and broke out completely because we didn't know when she would be gone. No one can wait for the death of their close loved ones. It's really challenging to see it coming. Our family never felt so helpless in our whole life. We have grown from null and even that moment didn't break our lives. **Death would arrive, but we didn't know when. It's pity to wait for the death of our own family member, especially of your own mother.** The dark night came, and as we all were exhausted, we decided to stay awake turn by turn for two hours each, so that everyone could get at least six hours of sleep. We initiated our turns, but as we all were mentally tired that even for a moment, our eyes were stealing the sleep. Unexpectedly, we all have fallen to sleep with partial consciousness. I remember, I remained next to my mother while holding her warm left hand.

Being a mother is too easy. Alright, I'm saying this because that's how we see our mother's care, duty and love as direct simple love; but being a son is too difficult when you have to return what your mother does for you for the whole life and expects nothing but some care and love. ***The son craves to return the debt to his mother for the whole life, accomplishes; complete yet incomplete.***

FIFTEEN

26TH AUGUST 2022

We plan everything, but it's the last step of God that decides what we were exactly planning for. Nothing is random in this world. Every move is pre-decided.

Suddenly at 3 o' clock, I woke up abruptly, but the reaction got lost in a moment as I saw my mother. Her eyes were completely open, and it happened after a period of six days. The tears rolled down my heavy eyes like I'm crying painfully right now while writing ahead. **It's the process of death. When someone is extremely close to death, they become unexpectedly active.** Sometimes you may feel like the person's health is improving, but now he's approaching death faster. After observing her wide-open eyes, I understood, her end was near. I called everyone and in a second, everyone started crying. To comfort her, we were pressing her hands and legs softly, doing massage on her head gently and praising her. It was a time when she was connecting with God. *We were praying, 'God, please take her in your shield.'* I had listened somewhere, when someone is very close to death, both the veils of earth and God get lifted,

and the person who is dying, can see both, and that's why they get unable to speak; otherwise, it would reveal all the secrets of God and death. Still, it was night and the time was around 5:30 AM. As the day could arrive anytime, she started to take reverse breaths like she was taking back all the breaths. It was excruciating to see that moment because it was a moment of someone's death. The tears were coming, but as we had been already crying for months, the tears had dried out like we had accepted the truth in a slow time. We were playing the Krishna Song, **Kanhaiya Le Chal Parli Paar**, which was her favourite song. Also, we played the songs that she remembered as her all-time favourites. I remembered every happy moment we felt together and we were sorry for if we did anything wrong to her. At 6 o' clock, we put Ganga Jal and Tulsi in her mouth. After five minutes, as the black blue sky came, she took her last breath. As she was unable to move even her tongue, it got dried and folded back near the throat. With her last breath, our vitals of the body fluctuated. We hugged each other in extreme unbearable pain and were trying to put ourselves in a situation where we could accept reality. She had gone into the shield of God. We looked around the room and realised that the room had only, the Krishna and Radha picture frames everywhere, and during her last time she only managed to chant some Krishna's mantra on Janmashtami. In her last time, she went to Raja Ram Temple to worship the Raja Ram. ***Everything was flashing in our eyes, and we realised, she actually went to heaven and at least now she was free from every pain.*** That was the only reason that has made our family so far on this painful journey. You know, **Hope is an extremely powerful energy and you can even cross the world's most tiring journeys with it.**

When I lost my mother, I held her hand for almost three days and it felt like a moment to be missed forever. With her death, I still have continuous ambivalent feelings to accept and deny the harsh truth, but when hearts ache, God listens, forgives, and transfers energy to accept any hard truth of life. *You know, true people live in good deeds even after death. Death is the chance for life to live forever in the hearts of people.*

One day, everything will die, and the whole world will get covered with nature just how my mother left plants on the terrace. When someone dies, the best growing thing they can leave is nature, to give back what they took from mother earth. When I wander in the garden cultivated by her, the soft touch of leaves reminds me of the gentle touch of her hands. *When someone dies, they leave a few things where their lived moments can be felt wholly. One day the whole world will die, and no one will know nothing. All the energies will die, and the emotions will vanish.*

Goodbyes hurt when the story isn't finished and the book has been closed. - jnd.

About The Author

www.authordeepakgupta.com

ABOUT THE AUTHOR

Deepak Gupta is pre-eminently known for writing plain sailing, meticulous, and pragmatic Self-Help books. He's the author of **more than forty books** including **10 Principles to Beat Failure** that won **Google Best Choice 2018** & became **Top Seller on Google Play Store in 2019**. He has been garnering much acclaim for his **30 Minutes Read & 10 Principles Series**. Till now, he has received **800k+ readership** & **a lot of appreciation** from all over the world. He believes in writing & living best exceptional content from his subconscious mind. He loves to observe, absorb, and write on various social issues, inspirational truthful words, short stories, and heart whelming poetry. Also, he has travelled to many places in India like Manali, Rajasthan, Goa, Kolkata, Madhya Pradesh, Jammu, Dalhousie, and Mussoorie to bring originality in his work. He *releases new short books every month* to get readers to connect with the truth of life.

Deepak Gupta received his post-graduation degree from **Delhi School of Economics**. Also, when he's not writing, he can be found wandering on his **exquisite terrace garden**. He lives with his family in **Delhi, India**.

Keep in touch with Deepak via the web:
Instagram @authordeepakgupta
Facebook: facebook.com/authordeepakgupta
Twitter @authordeepakgup

www.ingramcontent.com/pod-product-compliance
Lightning Source LLC
LaVergne TN
LVHW041632070526
838199LV00052B/3324